W9-AQR-404

SAMMY SPIDER'S
FIRST
WEDDING

KAR-BEN
PUBLISHING

To my grandchildren, Adler, Sascha, Eden, Leo, Derek and Hayden
—S.A.R.

For Ben and Lyn. Your marriage is Love Eternal.
—K.J.K.

KAR-BEN PUBLISHING, INC.
A division of Lerner Publishing Group, Inc.
241 First Avenue North
Minneapolis, MN 55401 USA
1-800-4-KARBEN

Website address: www.karben.com

Library of Congress Cataloging-in-Publication Data

Names: Rouss, Sylvia A., author. | Kahn, Katherine,
   illustrator.
Title: Sammy Spider's first wedding / by Sylvia A. Rouss ;
   illustrated by Katherine Janus Kahn.
Description: Minneapolis : Kar-Ben Publishing, [2019] | Series:
   Life cycle | Summary: Curious Sammy Spider becomes an
   unexpected guest at a wedding when the chuppah he is exploring
   gets carried to the synagogue for the ceremony and then to the
   reception hall.
Identifiers: LCCN 2018007303 (print) | LCCN 2018014496 (ebook) |
   ISBN 9781541542174 (eb pdf) | ISBN 9781512483666 (lb : alk. paper) |
   ISBN 9781512483673 (pb : alk. paper)
Subjects: | CYAC: Weddings—Fiction. | Judaism—Customs and practices—
   Fiction. | Spiders—Fiction.
Classification: LCC PZ7.R7622 (ebook) | LCC PZ7.R7622 Saem 2019 (print) |
   DDC [E]—dc23

LC record available at https://lccn.loc.gov/2018007303

Manufactured in the United States of America
1-43363-33175-4/12/2018

SAMMY SPIDER'S
FIRST
WEDDING

Sylvia A. Rouss

Illustrated by Katherine Janus Kahn

KAR-BEN
PUBLISHING

Sammy Spider gazed down from his web as Mr. Shapiro and Josh carried four large tree branches into the house.

"Mother, what are they doing with the branches?" asked Sammy.

"They're going to make a *chuppah* for their friend's wedding," answered Mrs. Spider. "The bride and groom will stand under it during the ceremony."

"Will we be going to the wedding too?" asked Sammy.

"Silly little Sammy!" laughed Mrs. Spider. "Spider's don't celebrate weddings. Spiders spin webs."

Sammy lowered himself onto one of the branches so he could get a closer look.

He watched Josh help Mrs. Shapiro attach a large *tallit* to the branches.

"It's beautiful," gasped Sammy.

The next day, Sammy was swinging happily from the branches on a piece of silk thread, when Josh and his parents came into the room all dressed up. Mr. Shapiro was holding something wrapped in a cloth napkin.

"What's in that napkin?" thought Sammy.

Mr. Shapiro carried the chuppah out the door. Mrs. Shapiro carried the flowers, followed by Josh carrying the little bundle.

Sammy slid down
onto the top of
the chuppah so he
could see better.

"Uh-oh! I guess
I'm going to the
wedding," said
Sammy.

At the synagogue, four guests held the branches of the chuppah during the beautiful wedding ceremony.

Sammy was excited
as he watched the
bride walk down the
aisle. Her lacy gown
reminded Sammy of
a giant spider web.

Sammy watched the bride walk
around the groom seven times.

The rabbi said the Kiddush, and the bride and groom sipped wine from a large cup. Sammy wanted a sip too, but he remembered that spiders don't celebrate weddings. Spiders spin webs.

Suddenly, Sammy
noticed the wrapped
bundle that Josh had
brought from home.

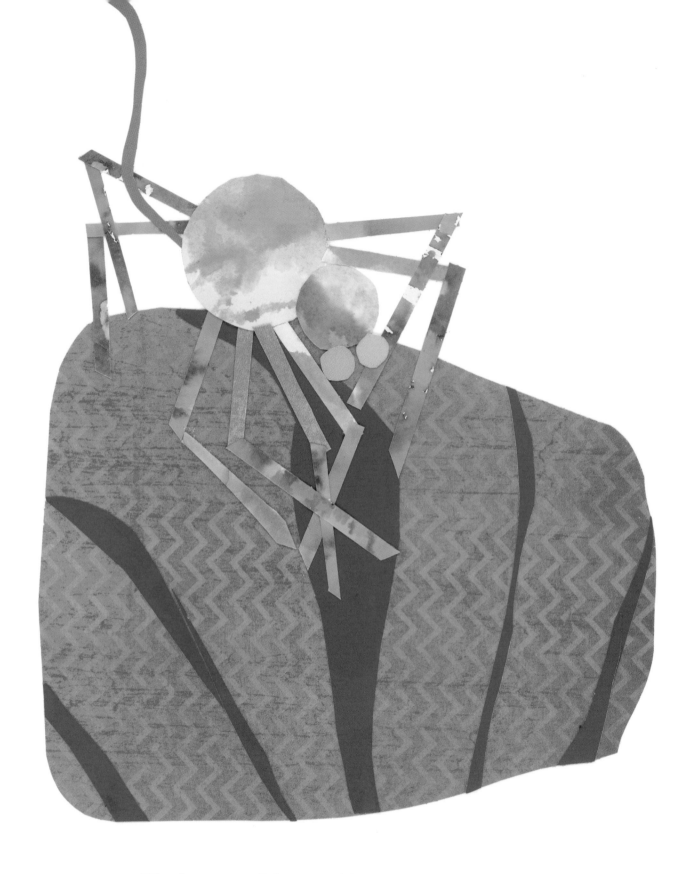

He lowered himself onto the table to
see what was inside the package.

He crawled into the folds of the napkin—and found himself in a wineglass. It was slippery. Sammy happily skated across it, laughing.

"Weddings are fun!" he giggled.

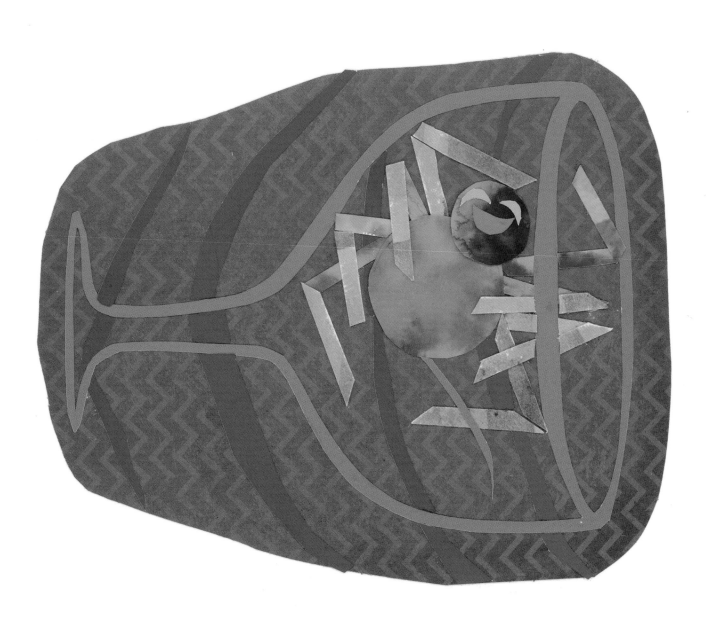

He peeked out from his hiding place and watched the groom place a gold ring on the bride's finger. Then the rabbi recited seven special blessings to honor the bride and groom. Sammy used his legs to count the blessings.

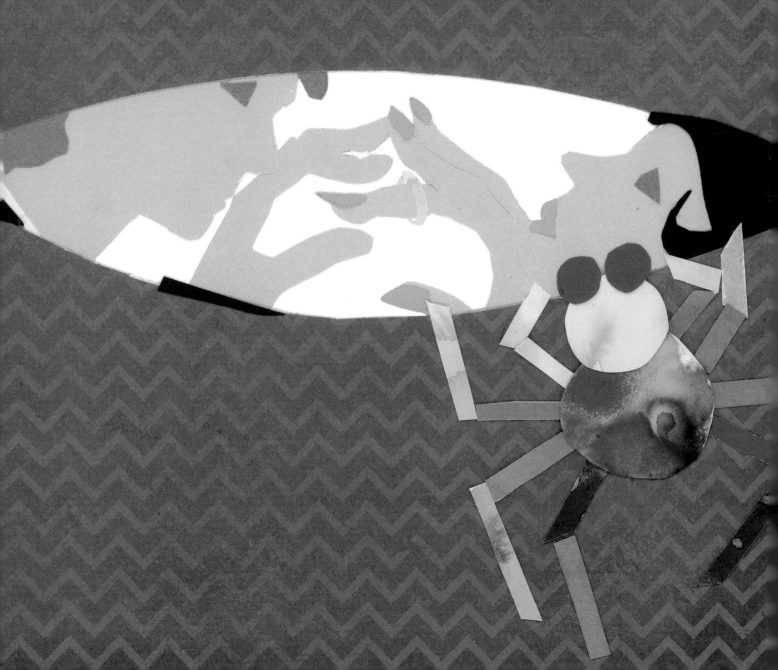

"I'm glad there are only seven blessings so I can count them on my legs!" thought Sammy.

Suddenly Sammy felt himself being lifted. The rabbi was placing the bundle with Sammy inside on the floor near the groom's foot. Then Sammy heard the rabbi say, "With the breaking of this glass, we remember that life has both happy moments and sad moments."

"Oh no!"

thought Sammy.

"The groom is going to stomp on this glass with me in it!"

Sammy struggled to get out of the glass, but his eight little legs were tangled inside. He tugged and pulled to free himself.

Above Sammy's head, the groom lifted his foot.
"Help!" Sammy shouted. He gave one final tug
and flew out of the napkin just as the groom's
heel came crashing down.

"SMASH!"

Sammy heard the glass shatter.

"MAZEL TOV!"

shouted the guests.

"PHEW!"

sighed Sammy.

He scurried back to the chuppah and climbed to the top. Around him, Sammy saw tables set for a festive meal with beautiful dishes and bowls of flowers on every table. He spotted a yummy wedding cake and heard music playing.

Sammy watched Josh and his parents join the other guests dancing the Hora.

The guests lifted the bride and groom in chairs and danced around them.

The party went so late
that Sammy fell asleep.
He woke up as the
Shapiros carried the
chuppah home.

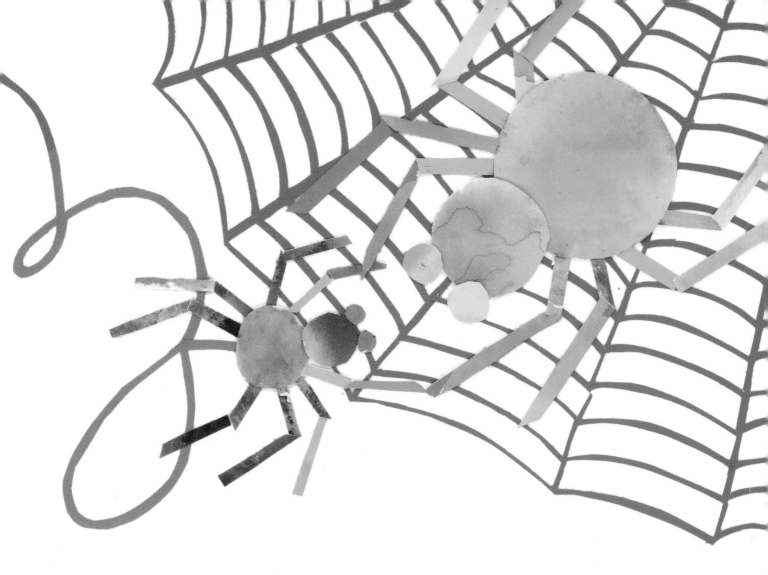

Excitedly Sammy climbed out of the chuppah and up to his web.

"Mother, I can't wait to tell you about the wedding celebration!" he exclaimed.

Mrs. Spider hugged him. "I want to hear all about it, Sammy. But first, it's time for our *webbing* celebration—that means it's bedtime for tired little spiders!"

About Jewish Wedding Customs

A Jewish wedding takes place under a chuppah, a wedding canopy. A symbol of the home the couple will create, it is open on four sides, recalling the tent of Abraham and Sarah, which was always open to guests. The wedding ceremony begins with the blessing over a cup of wine which the wedding couple shares. Seven special blessings are recited, praising God for the blessings of life and creation, and for the joy of the new couple. The breaking of the glass at the end of the ceremony has many meanings. Some say it is a reminder of the destruction of the Temple in Jerusalem. Others say it reminds us that even in the midst of great joy the world is not yet perfect. Guests shout "Mazel Tov!" at the end of a wedding ceremony to wish the new couple good luck.

Sylvia A. Rouss is an award-winning author and early childhood educator, and the creator of the popular **Sammy Spider** series, celebrating its 25th anniversary with over half a million Sammy Spider books sold. She lives in California.

Katherine Janus Kahn studied Fine Arts at the Bezalel School in Jerusalem and at the University of Iowa. She has illustrated many children's books including Kar-Ben's popular **Sammy Spider** series. She lives in Wheaton, Maryland.